THIS BOOK BELONGS TO ....

MY GIANT BOOK
OF BEDTIME STORIES

PUBLISHED BY PETER HADDOCK LIMITED, BRIDLINGTON, U.K.
Printed in USSR

CONTENTS

Puss~in~ Boots

Illustrations by J. L. MACIAS S.

Retold by JANE CARRUTH

There was once a poor miller who, when he died, left all he had to his three sons. The eldest had the mill, the second son had the donkey and Jack, the youngest, was left the cat.

"How can I earn my living with only a cat to help me?" Jack said sadly. "It is more likely we shall starve together, Puss."

"Do not be down-hearted, Master," said Puss. "Just get me a pair of tall boots and a sack and put your trust in me."

"Oh very well," said Jack. "But I don't see how you can help me."

As soon as he had the boots and the sack, Puss set out for the woods where he knew there were some very fine rabbits. After laying a trap for the rabbits by putting a fresh carrot inside his sack, he hid behind a tree, and it wasn't long before a rabbit came along.

No sooner was the plump little rabbit inside the sack than Puss pulled the string he was holding and the rabbit was caught. Now it was well known that the King simply adored rabbit pie and Puss headed straight for the palace. When he stood before the King, he said. "Your Majesty, my master, the Marquis of Carabas, has sent you a gift of a fine rabbit." The King was delighted with such a thoughtful gift and begged Puss-in-Boots to thank his noble master.

Puss-in-Boots went on catching rabbits and taking them to the King until he became quite a favourite at court. He soon learned that the King and the lovely Princess went for a drive in their coach at the same time each day. "You must bathe in the river close to the bridge," Puss told his master one morning. "I will hide your old clothes."

Greatly puzzled, Jack obeyed and was astonished to see Puss on the bridge and stopping the royal coach. "My master, the Marquis of Carabas has had all his fine clothes stolen," he told the King.

"He will have the best suit in my wardrobe," cried the King, and he sent a messenger back to the palace to fetch it. In his new clothes the miller's son looked very handsome and he was invited to ride in the coach with the lovely Princess. Meanwhile, Puss ran on ahead.

As soon as Puss came to a band of
workers in the fields, he said, "You
must tell the King that you work for
the noble Marquis of Carabas. If you
don't, I'll eat you up!"

19

Now Puss was making for a great castle where he knew a certain ogre lived. The ogre was very rich and very conceited. He was just about to sit down to his dinner when Puss-in-Boots arrived. "I hear," said Puss, "that you have wonderful powers. You can change yourself into a huge lion if you wish."

"That is very true," smiled the ogre. And did so immediately. Puss got such a fright that he scrambled up the nearest curtain and hung on for dear life, while the lion roared and snarled at him.

"Now I know you have truly wonderful powers," he was just able to squeak.

Then he went on, "It's easy for a great big fellow to turn himself into a great big lion. I wonder if you could change yourself into a tiny mouse? That must be too difficult for you!"

"Nothing easier," said the ogre, and did so at once.

Puss made a dive for the mouse and gobbled him up!

22

Now the castle was his, and Puss climbed the ramparts and waved his fine hat to stop the royal coach as it came clattering past. "Welcome, welcome!" he shouted. "Welcome to the castle of the noble Marquis of Carabas!"

No wonder the King began to think the Marquis must be a very rich man indeed!

23

In the great banqueting hall all was ready for a magnificent feast, and the miller's son, who had quite fallen in love with the Princess, led her to the table. The King and Puss-in-Boots watched the pair and both decided, almost at the same time, that it would be an excellent idea if they got married. After the feasting the young couple walked in the garden and Jack, the poor miller's son, proposed there and then to the Princess.

There was no happier young man in the whole world than Jack when the Princess declared her love for him. Puss-in-Boots was happy too. And, after the wedding, he was given a special velvet cushion of his own, and salmon and cream every day.

JULIE
and Michael's new puppy

Illustrations by José-Luis Macias S.
Original story by J. Barnabé Dauvister
Retold by Linda L. Booth

Michael thinks Julie is lucky to have a friend like Kitty.

Everywhere Julie goes Kitty is right beside her. She's a true
friend. I really would love to have a playmate like Kitty!

29

Wait a minute, you geese — I hear something crying.
Oh . . . a little puppy . . . it looks like he's been abandoned.

Let's stay with him to see if someone comes back for him. I hope no one does! What do you think, geese ... aren't we lucky we found each other? You must be hungry, my little friend.

I suppose we'll have to wait until tomorrow to find out if I can keep you. I want you to stay here with me on the farm . . . but how am I going to convince Mother?

"What are you going to call him. Michael?" asks Julie. "Fox!
Do you know when Mother will come back from shopping?"

Woof! Woof! Woof! Fox smells something. Look Michael, the pigs are helping themselves to our garden as though it's their own personal pantry.

Hurrah! Fox to the rescue. I think he'll be staying with us.
What a good dog! Did you hear him growl? Did you see
how he herded the pigs back to their pen?

Bravo, Fox! What a good watchdog you have proven
yourself to be. Mother will be delighted.

39

Michael is so happy. He doesn't have to watch the geese all
by himself now. On the way home from school Fox plays
with the geese and looks after his master.

Do you know what? We are going to grow up together, the
two of us. We'll share everything, you can count on
that . . . even our dreams.

Tom Thumb

Illustrations by J. L. MACIAS S.

Retold by JANE CARRUTH

There was once a woodcutter who had seven sons, the youngest being so tiny that he named him Tom Thumb. When the woodcutter could no longer feed his sons, he took them deep into the forest and left them.

The boys tried to find their way home, but when night fell they knew they were lost. Only little Tom Thumb kept up his spirits and it was he who discovered a huge castle which stood among the trees. "Come on, boys," he cried. "Don't be afraid!"

The woman who came to the castle door had a kind face, but when Tom Thumb asked her to give them food and shelter for the night, she looked afraid. "My husband is a terrible ogre," she said. "It would not be safe for you to stay here."
But Tom Thumb pleaded so hard that at last she let them come in.

They had no sooner sat down to supper when the ogre came home, and the woman had only time to hide the boys under the table before he strode into the kitchen.

"I smell fresh meat!" roared the ogre, and began searching the room. It wasn't long before he found the frightened boys and would have devoured them on the spot if his wife had not given him a big roast sheep to eat instead. "I'll eat them in the morning," he said. And his wife quickly put the boys to bed.

Their beds were in a room next to the ogre's seven daughters, who slept with gold crowns on their heads. That night, Tom Thumb crept into their room and put their crowns on the heads of his sleeping brothers. And it was just as well he did!

In the middle of the night, the wicked ogre stumbled upstairs. Tom Thumb was still wide awake and he heard the ogre mutter, "I must feel for the crowns of gold! I must not cut off the heads of my dear young daughters."

But that is just what the ogre did! It was too dark for him to see and when he touched the crowns he moved away from the boys' room into the room where his daughters were sleeping.

"Quick! We must escape now before the ogre finds what he has done!" Tom told his six brothers, and he led them down the wide stone stairs and out of the castle.

Once outside, they began to run, and they were a long way from the castle by morning. Now, when the ogre discovered what he had done, he fell into a black rage and pulling on his magic seven-league boots he set off in pursuit.

"Hide, hide!" whispered Tom, when suddenly they heard the crashing of branches. "The ogre is not far away." Tom Thumb showed his six frightened brothers where to hide just as the ogre thundered past, and they sighed with relief as he disappeared into the thick forest.

"Now we can follow him," said Tom Thumb bravely. "We shall be safer behind him than in front."

53

In his wonderful seven-league boots the ogre covered
many miles. But at last he grew weary and, stretching
himself out across a bridge he shut his eyes and was soon
fast asleep. "There he is," Tom Thumb whispered, when
at last the boys caught up with him. "And he has kicked off
one of his boots!"

Quickly, Tom told his brothers what he was going to do. "If we take his magic boots," he said, "the ogre will never catch us. Come on, boys, help me!" Tom began to tug at the other boot and his brothers joined in. How heavy it seemed. And how they pulled and tugged until it came off the giant's foot.

The seven-league boots, being magic, fitted anybody who put them on. And soon Tom Thumb was striding along in the ogre's boots, his brothers running and skipping behind. In no time at all their cottage was in sight and there was their mother!

How happy she was to see them again for she was sure
that they had been devoured by some wild forest animal.
"We must tell your father!" she cried at last. And when the
woodcutter came he wept tears of joy to have his children
safely home.

The king soon heard about Tom Thumb's adventures and
he was so pleased at his bravery that he appointed him
Royal Messenger. Tom Thumb, in his magic seven-league
boots, was the swiftest of Messengers, and it wasn't long
before his fortune was made!

Who Stole the Honey?

Illustrated by J.-L. Macias S.

In a cottage between the village and the wood live three children. Daniel is the eldest and he is looking after his two sisters while their parents are away. Pamela, the older sister, takes care of the house, and Nancy, the youngest, spends all her time reading. In the summer they pick fruit in the woods and collect logs for the long, hard winter.

Autumn is almost over. It is the right time to gather honey. "Tomorrow we will empty the hives to collect all the honey," says Daniel, as he prepares the masks. "Honey tastes delicious and is so good for coughs and colds."

But the next morning when they approach the
hives . . . "Oh no!" exclaims Pamela. "That bad bear is
ruining the hives." "Sssh!" replies Daniel. "Let's get out of
here – if the bear sees us he will attack. As soon as he has
eaten, he will go away."

"It's been a long time since the bear came to our part of the woods. He must be very hungry to come so close to our houses," says Daniel as he is making supper that night. When Pamela checks to see how much honey there is in the jar, she is surprised to find that there is almost none left.

As they are walking in the woods two days later, the children find
the big bear caught in a trap. Daniel sets him free.

68

The bear follows the children at a distance. He looks at them in a friendly way, as if to say thank you.

Early the next morning the little girls wake Daniel. They are very frightened. "There's a noise in the kitchen. The bear must have come into the house," says Pamela.

A broken jar is on the floor and someone has opened the door. But who?

Oh! What a surprise! It's the cat – the greedy cat – who has been eating the honey. Nancy is happy. The bear hasn't stolen anything.

"Now, let's go back to bed," says Daniel. "The bear
must have gone back to the mountain to spend the
winter in a warm cave."

Yes, the bear is almost asleep, but not very far away. He is
resting comfortably in the woodshed near the house. Nancy
will be so happy to see him.

Cinderella

Illustrations by J. L. MACIAS S.

Retold by JANE CARRUTH

Once upon a time there was a merchant who married again when his wife died. His new wife was a proud, cruel woman who hated the merchant's young daughter.

"Cinderella," she said, "will be her new name. Her place is in the kitchen, for she must do the work of a servant." The step-mother had two daughters. They were as proud and cruel as their mother, and very plain. At night they made poor Cinderella curl their hair and then sent her down to the kitchen to sleep on the stone floor, with only her faithful dog to keep her company as she slept.

Now, Cinderella, in her rags, was much prettier than the two Ugly Sisters. This made them very angry and, as the months passed, nothing she could do would please them. One day an invitation came from the palace to attend the Grand Ball the King was giving for his son, the Prince. Cinderella began to dream of going to the ball and this made the Sisters laugh at her.

"The Prince would never look at you in your rags!" they sneered. When at last the day came for the two Ugly Sisters to set out for the ball, Cinderella was at the washtub. "Oh, I do so long to be going to the Ball," she thought as she watched them go. And she sighed and began to cry because she was so sad at being left behind.

Still feeling sad, Cinderella set about the washing-up and it was then that something wonderful happened. Suddenly, there appeared before her the most beautiful lady she had ever seen. "I am your Fairy Godmother," said the beautiful lady.

"Do what I say and you will go to the Ball." Then she told Cinderella to take a big pumpkin outside and fetch her the mousetrap, which held six little mice. With a wave of her wand the Fairy changed the pumpkin into a magnificent golden coach.

The six little mice became six handsome horses and some garden
lizards found themselves changed into footmen. Cinderella
gasped when she saw that she was no longer in rags but in a
gorgeous dress of silk and satin embroidered with sparkling jewels
and that on her feet were two dainty glass slippers, the prettiest in
the world. "Am I dreaming?" she wondered.

82

"Remember," said the Fairy. "You must leave the Ball before the hour of midnight strikes or you will lose everything!"

As soon as Cinderella reached the palace, she was escorted into the ballroom. Almost at once, the King's son, the handsome young Prince, invited her to dance with him. All the ladies, who had hoped to dance with the Prince, were jealous.

84

"Who is she?" they whispered. "How lovely she looks! She must be a grand Princess. No wonder the Prince has eyes only for her!"

Cinderella was so happy dancing with the Prince that she forgot the Fairy's warning. The palace clock was striking the hour of twelve when she remembered. And with a cry of dismay she fled from the ballroom and down the palace steps.

In her haste, she left behind one of her pretty glass slippers. The Prince tried to follow her, but he saw only a poor young girl in rags running down the street followed by six little mice.

Day after day, the Prince thought only of his mysterious Princess. At last he sent out a Proclamation that he would marry the girl who could wear the dainty glass slipper. His Messengers would take the slipper to every house in the kingdom.

When the Royal Messenger arrived at Cinderella's house, the two
Ugly Sisters pushed and squeezed their feet into the slipper, but all
in vain. But when Cinderella tried on the slipper it proved a perfect
fit, and she was taken at once to the palace.

Cinderella and the Prince were married the very next day. Their wedding was the most magnificient the world had ever seen, and the happiest girl in the world was, of course, Cinderella.

Who Caught the Thieves?

Illustrated by J.-L. Macias S.

Pamela, Nancy and Daniel are so happy that their neighbour, Farmer Jackson, has promised to take them to a party in the meadow tomorrow. Pamela and Nancy are going to wear their best dresses. How nice of their neighbour to invite them!

The next morning everyone is ready on time. Mr. and Mrs. Jackson and their children have come to pick them up. "Good morning. Thank you for inviting us," says Pamela. "We are glad to have you with us," says Mr. Jackson. "Now come on everyone, let's get going – the party is waiting."

95

Everything at the party is so exciting for the three children, especially the little puppet theatre. Sweets and games are also part of the fun.

Daniel is very clever. He climbs to the top of the pole and wins . . . guess what . . . a beautiful live duck.

Nancy can't believe her eyes.
She is actually riding on a
merry-go-round, just like the
ones she has seen so often in
her picture books.

It's lunch time and everyone is very hungry. They discover a lovely spot at the foot of a tree and begin to eat. But before long a horseback rider arrives with bad news – some farms in the area have been robbed.

When our little friends arrive home they see an abandoned cart in front of their house. The front door has been forced open. The cart must belong to the thieves who have broken in. But where are they now?

Everyone jumps out of the wagon. "They must be inside, busy stealing," says Daniel. "Don't be afraid," Pamela comforts Nancy. "The thieves won't take anything from us."

Suddenly muffled noises and groans are heard inside the house and everyone hurries past the broken door to see what's happening. What a surprise! The table and chairs have been knocked over, the chest of drawers has been ransacked, a bag with some valuable objects has been left in the corner . . . and an angry big brown bear is looking up at two frightened burglars perched on top of a cupboard.

Everything ends happily. The policemen have taken the thieves away, and Nancy gives her friend, the bear, a big hug.

Little Red Riding Hood

Illustrations by J. L. MACIAS S.

Retold by JANE CARRUTH

Once upon a time there was a pretty little girl who lived with her Mummy and Daddy close to a big wood. Everybody called her Red Riding Hood because she always wore a red cape and hood.

On the far side of the big wood lived Red Riding Hood's grandmother and, one day, the little girl set out to visit her.

Little Red Riding Hood loved her grandmother and she was glad her Mummy had filled her basket with honey and cakes to take to her. Her Mummy had told her to go all the way around the wood because of the big bad wolf who lived there. But it was such a sunny day that Red Riding Hood forgot all about the wolf.

She went into the wood and, oh dear, quite soon she met that big bad wolf. "Good morning to you," said the wolf, in a soft, kind voice. "Where are you going?"

"To see my grandmother," said Red Riding Hood. "I'm taking her some honey and cakes because she isn't very well today."

The big bad wolf was very cunning. He pretended to be sad that Red Riding Hood's grandmother was not very well. And he soon found out just where she lived. "You gather some flowers to take to her," he said at last. "I must be off!"

Goodness, how fast that big bad wolf ran through the woods! He did not draw breath until he had found the grandmother's cottage and was knocking at the door. "It's your own Red Riding Hood," he called gently. "Unbolt the door and let me in."

No sooner was the wolf inside than he gobbled up the old lady. Then he wrapped her shawl around his shoulders, put on her pink nightcap and balanced her spectacles on his nose. "Now I'll wait for Red Riding Hood," he thought, as he jumped into bed.

He did not have long to wait. He had only time to pull the cover right up to his face before Red Riding Hood arrived.

"How are you?" she asked, going up to the bed. "I've brought you some pretty flowers and a basket full of good things."

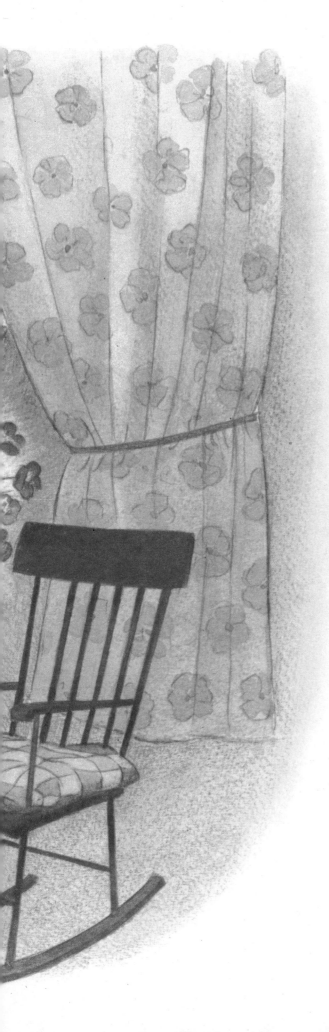

Then Red Riding Hood looked at her grandmother more closely, as the wolf croaked, "Come and give your Granny a kiss, child!"

"But Grandmama, what big ears you have got!"

"All the better to hear you with," said the wolf.

"And, oh Grandmama, what big eyes you have got."

"All the better to see you with," said the wolf.

"And Grandmama, what big teeth you have got!"

"All the better to eat you with," snarled the big bad wolf, and he sprang out of bed.

Poor little Red Riding Hood was so frightened that she dropped her basket and tried to escape. But the wolf caught her and gobbled her up.

Then he felt so heavy with the old lady and Red Riding Hood inside him that he climbed back into bed and fell asleep.

Now, two farm workers had seen the big bad wolf enter the old lady's cottage. "We had better go and find out if she is safe," they said to each other. Imagine their horror when they saw the wolf in bed and the room turned upside down. "The wolf has gobbled up the old lady for sure," said one.

"And the little girl," said the other. "We had better cut him open as fast as we can."

So the two brave men went into the cottage and they cut open the wolf, who was sleeping so heavily that he did not wake up, which was just as well, for out of his big stomach hopped the old lady and after her came little Red Riding Hood!

And while Red Riding Hood and her grandmother ran outside to hide in the woods, the two farm workers filled the wolf's stomach with heavy stones and then sewed it up.

When the big bad wolf did wake up he felt so heavy and thirsty that he staggered out of the cottage and made his way to the pond for a drink. But the stones moved inside his stomach. He over-balanced and fell into the water and soon drowned.

When the old lady heard the wolf was dead, she took Red Riding Hood back to the cottage. She hugged and kissed the little girl and said that all the excitement had made her feel much better. Then they tidied up the room and had cakes and honey for tea. So, after all, it was a happy day for them both.

JULIE
and her new hat

Illustrations by José-Luis Macias S.
Original story by J. Barnabé Dauvister
Retold by Linda L. Booth

I love my new hat. It's perfect for the school fair.

Oh Muffin, look, mushrooms . . . the first of the year. Let's take them back to Grandmother; she loves them. But what will we carry them in?

I have an idea – my new hat makes a perfect mushroom basket! Let's pack them carefully. Remember, we never, never taste a mushroom until we've brought them all home for Grandmother to check. Some mushrooms are poisonous.

Woof! Woof!
What is it now, Muffin? I'll be right there.
Poor little turtle. How have you rocked over on your back?
Isn't it lucky that Muffin saw you?

There you are, saved. But on your merry way, turtle.
Woof, woof! What is it now Muffin?

"Uh oh . . . leave those mushrooms alone, you rascals. They aren't for you!" Muffin is so intent on saving the harvest that he darts out after the badgers . . .

. . . knocking Julie into the brook!

Such greedy scoundrels! The badgers have no interest in sharing with Grandmother. Muffin is furious, and bravely puts up a very good fight.

What a sad state of affairs! No more mushrooms for Grandmother. Look at Julie's pretty dress . . . and, oh no, her new hat. "I can't possibly go to the fair like this," say Julie.

"Oh Julie, what happened to you?"
"Please don't ask . . . I'm so disappointed . . .

It's a long story, but it was all because of some beautiful mushrooms . . ."

You are the hero of this adventure, my little Muffin. I am so proud to have such a courageous friend!

The Sleeping Beauty

Illustrations by J. L. MACIAS S.

Retold by JANE CARRUTH

Once upon a time there lived a King and Queen who longed, with all their hearts, for a child of their own.

After many years, and to their great joy, the Queen gave birth to a beautiful baby girl. All the people rejoiced with them.

"We must invite all our friends to the Christening Party," said the Queen. "And we must invite all the fairies."
Alas, the King forgot to send an invitation to one of the oldest and most important fairies in the land and so he had no special present made for her.

142

The fairies who came to the Christening bestowed upon the baby many wonderful gifts. Beauty and grace and intelligence would all be hers as she grew up. Then, suddenly, the oldest fairy in the land appeared, dressed in black and with a face twisted in rage. "I, too, have a gift for the royal baby!" she screamed. "She will die from the prick of a spindle when she is fifteen years old!" And she laughed loudly.

143

Now the youngest of the fairies had not yet bestowed her gift on the little Princess.

"Be of good heart," she told the horrified King and Queen. "The child will not die. She will fall into a deep sleep which will last one hundred years, and then a king's son shall wake her." But the royal parents could not be comforted and the King said that every spindle in the land must be burned. Any person caught using a spinning wheel would be put to death.

Years passed and the Princess grew into a beautiful young girl, greatly loved by all who knew her. On her fifteenth birthday her parents took her to their castle in the country, where she was free to walk and play in the gardens, and ride her pony along country lanes.

One day, the Princess set out to explore all the small rooms at the very top of the castle. In one, she came upon an old woman, busy spinning. "Let me try, good mother!" she cried.

146

Now the old woman had not heard of the wicked fairy's curse or even that the King had a daughter. "Take it then, my pretty child," she said, handing her spindle to the Princess. Almost at once the girl felt a sharp prick and, with a small cry, she fell to the ground and lay as if dead. Terrified, the old woman rushed from her turret room, shouting for help.

Sadly, the King and Queen told their servants to carry the Princess to her bed-chamber. Then a strange thing happened.

148

All who were in the castle that day fell into a deep sleep. Even the cats and dogs and the little doves went to sleep.

149

This was the work of the youngest fairy, who came to the castle in her chariot drawn by dragons. So powerful was her magic that even the cook fell asleep in the very act of tasting the soup, and the jesters in the middle of telling jokes! One hundred years passed and all around the castle had grown a thick hedge of briars and thorns.

One day, a king's son was hunting in the forest and when he heard the story from an old woodcutter of the Sleeping Beauty in the strange, silent castle, he made up his mind to cut through the thick hedge and break into the castle so that he might find out for himself if the story was true.

The Prince drew his sword, but it was not needed, for a path appeared and he had only to follow it to reach the castle gates.

All was still and silent as the young Prince began his search for the Sleeping Beauty. He came upon her as last, lying on a bed of silver, her golden hair spread about her shoulders. And so lovely was she that the Prince lost his heart to her.

"So the story of the Sleeping Beauty is true," he said to himself, as he stood gazing at her. "How wonderfully beautiful she is!" Slowly, he approached the bed. Then he bent down and gently kissed the Princess. At the touch of his lips, she opened her eyes, and the sleeping castle came to bustling life.

The Princess, on waking, knew that she too had found her true love and the very next day they were married. So beautiful did she look on her Wedding Day that the Prince did not even notice that her wedding gown was one hundred years out of fashion!

Who Saved the Day?

Illustrated by J.-L. Macias S.

Autumn is almost over. Soon it will be winter and the countryside will be covered in snow. Daniel, Pamela and Nancy have decided to go fishing. They are going to the nearby river with some friends. Daniel is very proud of his new fishing rod. "We don't need to bring anything to eat," he says. "We'll catch enough fish to feed everyone."

The children arrive at the fishing spot opposite the tiny
cottage where John the forester lives. John and his dog
have come out to greet them. "You are here on a good
fishing day," he tells them. "It rained very hard last
night, and by tomorrow the muddy water will have run
down the river and the fish will hide away under the
rocks."

They catch lots of fish. Cliff decides to cook the fish himself. "You see, Pamela," he says proudly, "there are enough fish for all of us." Everyone is happy, but David notices that the old forester and his dog are staring up at the mountain.

Suddenly the woods become silent. The dog senses
danger, but what can it be? Everything is too quiet. The
birds have stopped singing . . . not a sound is heard. All of
the wild animals have disappeared. One little squirrel
hurries past as fast as he can. What is happening?

Then the scary silence in the forest changes to a terrifying
noise of broken branches, and suddenly a torrent of water
rushes down the mountain. It is the rain water from last
night which has been trapped in a dam of fallen branches
and stones, and now everything is breaking loose.

164

It all happens so fast. The muddy water rushes
towards the river. "Quick, children!" cries the old forester.
"The water will rise dangerously!" Everyone runs for safety
up the mountain, except for Nancy and one little boy. They
are in a boat which is being carried away by the river's
current. "Help!" cries Nancy. "I must get to them before
they reach the rapids!" Daniel shouts as he quickly jumps
on his horse.

Daniel hurriedly gallops on his horse, but he can't catch up with the boat. The current is getting swifter and it is carrying the little boat towards the dangerous rapids.

It seems too late to help. But then suddenly a big brown
bear appears on a tree trunk that has fallen into the river.
Nancy recognizes him and cries "Cuddles! Cuddles!
Help! Help!"

In a few moments the bear gently picks up the children in his paws and brings them to safety just as the little boat is pulled wildly down the river by the current.

Daniel watches anxiously from a distance. Nancy, so happy that she and her little friend have been rescued, runs towards her brother crying, "You saw what happened, didn't you? Cuddles saved us both!"

Everyone congratulates the brown bear for his bravery, but he does not stay long with the children. Winter is not far off, and he must search for a shelter in which to hibernate. "Goodbye, Cuddles," shouts Nancy as he goes off. "You'll be back in the spring, won't you?"

Snow-White
and the 7 Dwarfs

Illustrations by J. L. MACIAS S.

Retold by JANE CARRUTH

Once upon a time there was a young Princess called Snow-White whose mother had died soon after she was born.

Snow-White's father, the King, married again. His new Queen was a strange woman, tall and beautiful, but with the powers of a witch. In a secret room at the top of the palace were hidden her Book of Magic Spells, her raven and her black pot of magic potions.

On the wall hung a magic mirror. Every day, the Queen looked into her magic mirror and asked it the same question: "Mirror, mirror on the wall, who is the fairest of us all?" And the mirror would reply: "You, O Queen, are the fairest of all."

Then one day, the magic mirror
told the proud Queen that
Snow-White was now the fairest
in the land. "Then she must die!" cried the Queen in a rage. And she sent for
one of her huntsmen and told him to take the girl into the forest and kill her.
But the huntsman could not do such a cruel thing.

174

He told Snow-White to hide away in the forest. Soon after he left her, Snow-White came upon a little cottage among the trees. When she opened the door and looked inside, she saw seven little chairs around the untidy breakfast table.

In the room upstairs, Snow-White found seven little beds and, with a huge yawn, she lay down and was soon fast asleep. She was still asleep when the seven little dwarfs came home from the gold and diamond mines where they worked. How surprised they were to find Snow-White in their cottage.

"Who can she be?" they asked each other in wonderment.

The dwarfs waited patiently until Snow-White opened her eyes. When they heard her sad story, the eldest said, "You may stay here if you promise to cook for us and keep the cottage tidy."

"I should love to," said Snow-White. And from that day she became the dwarfs' housekeeper and took care of them.

Now the wicked Queen soon learned from her magic mirror that Snow-White still lived and, disguising herself as an old country woman, she hurried to the cottage. "I have brought you a lovely rosy-red apple, pretty one," she croaked when she saw Snow-White.
Alas, the apple contained a deadly poison.

No sooner did Snow-White take a bite of the poisoned apple than she fell to the ground. The seven dwarfs wept bitter tears when they came home from the mines and found her.

"This is the work of the evil Queen," said one, shaking his head. "She is too beautiful to lie buried in the cold earth," said another. "Let us make her a glass coffin so that all who pass this way may see how beautiful she is!"

And that is what the seven sad little dwarfs did! Day and night, two sat by the glass coffin on guard until, one day, a handsome Prince came riding through the forest.

The Prince fell so deeply in love with Snow-White that he begged the dwarfs to allow his servants to take her back to his palace. And, at last, they agreed. But when the glass coffin was moved the piece of poisoned apple, lodged in her throat, fell from her mouth. She was alive! Overcome with joy, the Prince told Snow-White that he loved her with all his heart.

Soon after, the noble Prince carried Snow-White away on his white charger. The seven little dwarfs were sad to see her go, but when they attended her wedding the next week, they danced for joy!

186

Who Ate the Biscuits?

Illustrated by J.-L. Macias S.

It's Christmas time. Pamela, Daniel and Nancy are so happy because the children from the nearby farm are coming to spend the holidays with them. They are all friends and go to the same school. Their names are Cathy, Diana, Mark, and their little cousin Bobby, who takes his violin everywhere he goes. The guests have brought all sorts of good things to eat. Daniel and Nancy go out to welcome their friends, but Pamela is very busy making some delicious biscuits for dessert.

Soon the children go out to look for a Christmas tree for the front of the house. They want a really big, beautiful one. Daniel has an axe to cut the tree down. They also bring along two sledges which Cathy, Diana, Nancy and Bobby try to ride. Again and again they fall off the sledges, but no one is hurt. Everyone is laughing and having so much fun.

At last they find a beautiful tree. The children are so happy!
They put the tree on one of the sledges, and a big bundle of
wood on the other.

It's time to go back home. The sledge rides are over for today and the children have enjoyed themselves, playing in the snow.

The children place the tree in front of the house while Pamela takes the biscuits out of the oven and puts them on the windowsill to cool. Everyone must wait until after supper to eat them.

Now the children start to trim the tree. Lanterns, garlands and brightly coloured paper chains the children have made themselves come out of the box and gaily decorate the tree.

Nancy and her friends decide to have a snowball fight while they wait for supper. Suddenly Pamela, looking a little angry and carrying a half-empty biscuit tray, orders everyone back to the house. The children stop throwing snowballs and quietly go back to the house.

"Someone just couldn't wait for supper," says Pamela. "I see some biscuits are missing." Then she says, "And if you eat too many of these biscuits, your hair will turn green!"

To everyone's surprise Bobby rushes to the mirror and pulls off his hat. He is so relieved to discover that his hair is not green. Of course, it was just Pamela's trick to see who stole the biscuits.

Bobby promises to be good in the future, and not to be selfish and help himself before the others. Pamela suggests that they all go out and sing carols under the tree before supper. In a few minutes the children are outside playing their own musical instruments.

Bobby plays his violin. The greedy little boy who took the biscuits has now become a wonderful musician. The other children are very pleased to hear how well Bobby plays. They are all quiet as they listen to him. It is a very special moment.

When Bobby has finished playing the children congratulate him.
"Oh, Bobby!" cries Nancy. "If you want to you can have my share
of the biscuits. A musician like you deserves them." Everyone
laughs. It has begun to snow so they go back into the house where
a delicious supper is waiting for them. Perhaps Bobby will play his
violin again. . . .

THE END